JOIN THE FUN
IN CABIN SIX . . .

KATIE is the perfect team player. She loves competitive games, planned activities, and coming up with her own great ideas.

MEGAN would rather lose herself in fantasyland than get into organized fun.

SARAH would be much happier if she could spend her time reading instead of exerting herself.

ERIN is much more interested in boys, clothes, and makeup than in playing kids' games at camp.

TRINA hates conflicts. She just wants everyone to be happy . . .

AND THEY ARE! Despite all their differences, the Cabin Six bunch are having the time of their lives at CAMP SUNNYSIDE!

Look for More Fun and Games with
CAMP SUNNYSIDE FRIENDS
by Marilyn Kaye
from Avon Books

Coming Soon

MARILYN KAYE is the author of many popular books for young readers, including the "Out of This World" series and the "Sisters" books. She is an associate professor at St. John's University and lives in Brooklyn, New York.

Camp Sunnyside is the camp Marilyn Kaye wishes that she had gone to every summer when she was a kid.

Happily Ever After

Marilyn Kaye

AN AVON  CAMELOT BOOK

CAMP SUNNYSIDE FRIENDS #16: HAPPILY EVER AFTER is an original publication of Avon Books. This work has never before appeared in book form.

AVON BOOKS
A division of
The Hearst Corporation
1350 Avenue of the Americas
New York, New York 10019

First Avon Camelot Printing: February 1992

CAMELOT TRADEMARK REG. U.S. PAT. OFF. AND IN OTHER COUNTRIES, MARCA REGISTRADA, HECHO EN U.S.A.

Printed in the U.S.A.

OPM 10 9 8 7 6 5 4 3 2 1

For Marie-Emmanuelle Amphoux

Chapter 1

Sarah Fine lay on her bed, reading. The mystery she'd checked out of the library just the day before was fantastic, full of twists and surprises that kept her guessing. She'd stayed up way past her bedtime because she couldn't put the book down. In fact, she'd actually fallen asleep with the open book beside her on the pillow!

All that day, at school, she read every chance she got—during library period, at lunch, and she even managed to sneak in a few pages in the classroom, hiding the mystery in her textbook so the teacher wouldn't see it.

Now, she was in the last chapter, and she didn't want it to end. She tried not to read too fast, but she couldn't help herself. It was so exciting! Any second now, the true villain would be revealed! She raced through the last few pages. Then, with a deep sigh of satisfaction and a little regret, she put the book down.

Sarah hated when she finished a really good book. She made a note of the author's name. She'd have to look for more of her books in the library.

But it was too late to go to the library now. And it was too early for dinner. She didn't feel like starting her homework yet, and she knew there was nothing good on television.

On her desk, an open envelope caught her eye. It was a letter from her older sister, Alison, who was away at college. Sarah had received it and read it a week ago. She was long overdue to write back.

She went to her desk and pulled out a sheet of her best flowered stationery. *Dear Alison,* she wrote. *How are you? I'm fine.*

Now what? she wondered. For someone who wanted to be a writer someday, she had a hard time writing letters—at least, from home. It wasn't difficult at all writing letters home in the summer, when she was away at Camp Sunnyside. There were always lots of activities to report, and news about her cabin mates. But home life was pretty much a routine.

She thought about what Alison had written

2

in her last letter and started to write. *Congratulations on the A you got on your term paper,* she scribbled. *I didn't understand the subject, but I'm sure you were brilliant! That guy you're going out with sounds really cool. Hang on to him!*

Now it was time to tell Alison what was going on in *her* life. She *could* tell her about this book she'd just finished. But then she thought of something more interesting.

Everything's fine here. But Dad's been acting strange. Not bad, just weird. He goes around whistling, sometimes even singing! And he's been daydreaming, with this really goofy smile on his face.

She paused, and conjured up an image of her father before he'd begun acting odd. Dr. Fine was usually a pretty serious man. He was kind, of course, and always willing to listen to his daughters. But he definitely wasn't the type to whistle or daydream with a goofy smile. And there was more to his behavior than that. He was just plain different. How could she describe this to her sister?

Dad is happy, she wrote. *And I think I know why. Remember my friend Trina Sandburg from camp? You know how Dad met Trina's mother*

3

during a Parents' Day. And you know that Mrs. Sandburg wrote an article about Dad's medical research for a magazine. They got together a lot for that. But even after the article was finished, they kept on getting together. And personally, I think they're getting to be more than just friends.

Her thoughts went back to a week earlier, when she and her father had met Trina and Mrs. Sandburg for dinner in a restaurant in a town halfway between the towns they lived in. The girls had gone to the salad bar. Suddenly, Trina had elbowed her. "Look," she'd said.

Sarah had glanced back at the table. Her father and Trina's mother were holding hands. "Maybe he's taking her pulse," she'd suggested to Trina. "He *is* a doctor."

Trina giggled. "But she's not his patient."

At that moment, their parents had looked up and seen them. Quickly, they'd dropped each other's hands. Yes, something was definitely going on.

A glance at the clock brought Sarah back to the present. It was time to get dinner started. She'd have to finish the letter later.

The Fines had a part-time housekeeper, Mrs. Blake, who prepared dinners for them on the evenings that Dr. Fine worked late at the hospital. Usually, she left some sort of a casserole for Sarah to stick in the oven. Walking into the kitchen, Sarah opened the refrigerator and found it.

Peeking under the lid, she wrinkled her nose in distaste. It was that chicken and broccoli thing with the gooey mushroom soup on top. She turned the oven on to preheat and collected plates to set the table.

It was quiet in the house. Sarah thought about her friend Karen whose house was never quiet. Karen had two parents, a sister, a brother, and a grandmother. Her house was always noisy, with people running around and calling to each other. Sometimes it was fun being there. But Sarah was always happy to come back to her own quiet, peaceful home.

She jumped when she heard the door slam. The bang was followed by some off-key singing. Seconds later, her father appeared in the kitchen.

"Hiya, pumpkin," he sang out.

"Dad! You're early!" Sarah exclaimed. "You never get home till seven on Thursdays." Usually, when Dr. Fine finished seeing patients, he went to his office and looked through his mail. Sarah had heard his friends call him a workaholic.

5

"Just didn't feel like hanging around the office today," he replied. "What's for dinner?"

"Mrs. Blake left that chicken and broccoli casserole thing," Sarah told him.

Dr. Fine didn't look any more thrilled with that than Sarah was. "I've got a better idea," he said. "Let's send out for pizza!"

Sarah was startled, almost shocked. If there was one thing she knew for sure about her father, it was the fact that he liked his routine. Sending out for pizza was something they did on Sunday evenings. On Thursdays, they ate Mrs. Blake's casseroles, no matter what they were.

"What's wrong?" her father asked. "Don't you want pizza?"

Sarah found her voice. "Sure I do!" She turned off the oven and put the casserole back in the refrigerator.

"You call the pizza place," he instructed her. "I'm going to change my clothes."

Still feeling a little confused, Sarah went to the phone, dialed, and ordered the pizza. By the time her father returned to the kitchen, she had pretty much recovered from her shock. But when she saw what he had on, she was stunned again. "Dad! You're wearing jeans!"

He chuckled, a little self-consciously. "I picked them up on the way home. What do you think? Do I look silly?"

"Heck no," Sarah replied. "You look great." She gazed at him in wonderment. Her father had never paid much attention to his appearance before. His clothes were always neat and clean, but nobody would ever call them fashionable. Suddenly, he seemed very concerned about his appearance.

He started singing under his breath as he went to the refrigerator and got out some orange juice. It dawned on Sarah that she recognized the tune. "Dad, that's a Billy Joel song."

"I know."

"But—you *hate* rock music!"

"Oh, some of it isn't so bad."

A memory hit Sarah. Back when her father had visited Camp Sunnyside, he and Trina's mother had talked about music, and Mrs. Sandburg had defended the merits of rock to Dr. Fine, who listened only to classical music.

"Since when did you start listening to Billy Joel?" Sarah demanded.

"Well, Laura played this record . . ."

"Laura?"

A hint of red crept up her father's neck. "Mrs. Sandburg."

Sarah studied her father with interest. She'd never seen him blush before.

The doorbell rang. "That must be the pizza," Sarah said. She followed her father to the front door. As he paid the delivery boy, Sarah took the pizza and carried it to the dining room table. She laid out plates and napkins, and opened the box. The spicy aroma rose up to greet her.

"Mm, c'mon Dad, let's eat."

There was no response, and she turned. "Dad?"

He was standing by the sideboard, where a collection of framed family photos stood. One photo was in his hand.

Sarah stood by him, and looked at the picture of the pretty, dark-haired woman. It was odd to think that this stranger had been her mother. Sarah had been only a baby when she died.

"You don't remember your mother," Dr. Fine murmured. "She was a very fine person."

Sarah touched his arm. "Dad? Is something wrong?"

"No, no." He replaced the photo, and sat down at the table. Sarah served him a slice of pizza. But her father didn't begin eating right away.

"Sarah, you like Laura ... Mrs. Sandburg, don't you?"

"Sure." Sarah picked up a piece of pizza and took a bite. "She's cool."

"Mm ... I think so too."

"And pretty," Sarah added.

"Yes, very pretty," her father agreed.

"And nice, and cheerful, and she's got a great sense of humor," Sarah said.

Her father nodded.

"You know what I think, Dad?"

"What?"

Sarah took a deep breath. "I think you're in love."

She didn't know what she was enjoying more—the pizza ... or the expression on her father's face.

Trina Sandburg opened the door of her father's car. Ignoring the bite of the cold February wind, she leaned over and kissed his cheek. "That was a great shopping trip, Dad. Thanks a lot. And thank Shelly for me too, okay?"

"Absolutely, sweetie," her father replied. "See you this weekend!"

Trina slammed the door shut and waved as

her father began backing out of the driveway. Her father and Shelly had been married almost a month now. At first, Trina hadn't been too thrilled about it. Ever since her parents' divorce, she'd harbored a secret wish that they'd get back together. She'd schemed and plotted and held on to her hope. And she'd resented Shelly for shattering that hope.

With some embarrassment, she remembered the first time she'd met Shelly, before the marriage. Her father had brought his girlfriend up to Camp Sunnyside to meet Trina. Trina hadn't exactly been rude—but she certainly hadn't been very friendly to the woman either.

But after spending more time with her after she got home from camp, Trina realized how wrong she'd been, not just about Shelly but about everything. She could see that even if her father had never met another woman, he and her mother were never going to get married again. They had changed over the years, and they just weren't right for each other anymore. That's the way it was, and Trina was going to have to accept it.

Besides, after getting to know her, Trina could see that Shelly was a nice person. Trina had never seen her father look happier than he was looking now. They lived close by, so Trina was able to see them often, not just on weekends.

Come to think of it, she'd never seen her mother look happier either. Mrs. Sandburg was always good-natured, but lately there had been a new light in her eyes. And Trina had a feeling she knew who was putting it there.

Her father's car was still poised at the end of the driveway, and Trina knew it would remain there until she was safely inside the apartment building. Waving again, she ran inside. She passed up the elevator and walked up the three flights. She was just about to hit the doorbell when she decided she'd better not tear her mother away from her work. So she fished around in her backpack for her key.

Once inside the apartment, a small sigh escaped her lips. The place looked so dark and cramped after the bright, airy house her father and Shelly had moved into. Every now and then, her mother talked about leaving the apartment and moving into a house. But she was a freelance writer, and lately, she'd been getting a lot of writing assignments. She worked very hard, and she always seemed to be under pressure.

There was never any time to go out and look at places.

Right this moment, she was probably banging away at her personal computer, frantically pounding out an article to meet some magazine or newspaper deadline. Trina tiptoed down the hall toward her mother's tiny office.

As she drew nearer, she heard music, which was odd because her mother usually liked complete silence while she wrote. Trina's eyes widened as she stood in the office doorway. Her mother didn't look frantic at all. From a small cassette player, strains of a concerto filled the air. The screen of the personal computer was blank. Mrs. Sandburg was leaning back in her chair, her eyes closed, a small, dreamy smile on her face.

"Mom?"

Trina spoke softly, but her mother jumped.

"Trina! You startled me!"

"I'm sorry."

"That's all right. I was off on a cloud somewhere. Did you have a good time shopping with your father and Shelly?"

"It was super," Trina said with enthusiasm. "Shelly's got the most fantastic taste! Look at what I got." From a bag, she pulled out a skirt and a sweater. "She matched these for me. I would never have thought to put these together. We stopped for sundaes, and we talked and talked, about everything!"

Suddenly, she clapped a hand to her mouth. How could she ramble on like this about how wonderful her father's new wife was? What would her mother think?

"Oh, Mom, I hope you don't think . . . I mean, Shelly's neat and all that. But more like a friend. Not like a mother. Not like you."

Mrs. Sandburg's smile was warm and steady. "Darling, I'm *glad* you like Shelly, I *want* you to like her. You know, some kids have a hard time accepting stepparents. But you've been wonderfully mature about this. It makes me happy, knowing you don't mind the idea of having stepparents."

She did look pleased. Almost too pleased. Trina cocked her head to one side and eyed her mother mischievously. "You keep saying stepparents, plural. Like maybe I'm going to get another one."

She wasn't alarmed by the fact that her mother's cheeks were getting very pink. Maybe Mrs.

Sandburg thought her daughter was still a little girl. But Trina had eyes and ears. And as her mother said, she was mature. She knew what was going on.

Her mother made a feeble effort to look surprised and innocent. "What makes you say that?"

Trina grinned. "Come on, Mom. You've been going out with Dr. Fine for six months. I've seen the way you fuss with your hair and your makeup and your clothes every time he's on his way here. *And* I've seen the way you look at him. You like him."

"Well, of course I like him."

"I don't mean just 'like.' I mean *like.*"

Mrs. Sandburg gave up her attempts to play dumb. She threw back her head and laughed. "I can't hide anything from you, can I? Not that I'd want to." She reached out, took Trina's hands, and pulled her closer.

"Tell me, Trina. What do you think of Martin? Dr. Fine, I mean."

"He's great," Trina said promptly. "He's friendly, and he's smart, and he doesn't talk to me like I'm a baby. What do *you* think of him? That's the important question."

14

That soft, dreamy smile reappeared on her mother's face. "You're right, Trina. I do like him. A lot. He's the most interesting man I've ever known. He's kind and he's gentle and he's truly caring. I feel totally comfortable with him, as if I've known him all my life."

"I know he feels the same way about you," Trina said.

"How do you know that?"

"Because I've seen the way *he* looks at *you!*"

Mrs. Sandburg giggled. For a moment, she looked exactly like a teenager. "I've asked Dr. Fine and Sarah over for dinner Sunday evening."

Trina gaped. "You're going to cook for him?"

Mrs. Sandburg nodded.

"Mom, he's a gourmet cook! And you're—"

Her mother interrupted, her eyes twinkling. "Are you saying I'm not very talented in that department?"

It was an old joke between them. "Oh, nothing like that," Trina said. "But if you really like this man, maybe it's not such a good idea to poison him."

"Oh, you!" Mrs. Sandburg pretended to take a swipe at her, and they both dissolved into gales of laughter. But even as she giggled, Trina made a mental note to be back early from her father's on Sunday—just in case she was needed to do some major rescue work in the kitchen!

Chapter 2

"Why do you have to get back so early?" Trina's father asked as they drove back to the apartment building Sunday afternoon.

"A friend of mine is coming over for dinner. Sarah Fine, from Camp Sunnyside." Trina paused. "Her father's coming too."

Mr. Sandburg's eyebrows went up slightly. "Her father?"

"Yes. Dr. Fine and Mom are . . . friends."

His eyebrows rose even higher. "Good friends?"

"Very good," Trina replied. "Um, I think they might be even more than friends."

A slow smile spread across her father's face. "That's good news." He sounded genuinely pleased. Stopping at a red light, he turned to Trina. "I hope you think so too."

17

"Oh, I *do*," Trina said fervently. "Dr. Fine's a very nice man."

Keeping one hand on the steering wheel, Mr. Sandburg reached over and ruffled Trina's short, dark hair with the other. "You're a good daughter, Trina. Your mother and I are very lucky to have you."

Trina beamed. There was nothing in the world she liked better than to have everyone around her happy.

When she entered the apartment, she sniffed. There were no smells of cooking in the air, but at least she couldn't smell anything burning. "Mom! I'm home!"

There was no reply. Trina hurried into the kitchen. There, she gazed in dismay at the ingredients spread out on a counter. The chicken didn't worry her. But there was a strange-looking, large orange fruit she didn't recognize, a carton of yogurt, and a bunch of spices she'd never heard of—coriander, cumin, turmeric. What in the world was her mother planning to make?

She heard the front door slam. "I'm in here, Mom," she called out.

A second later, her mother breezed in, a bag in her arms. A bunch of flowers and a long loaf

18

of french bread stuck out of the top. "Let me help you," Trina said, taking the bag.

"Thanks, darling," her mother said breathlessly. "I had to run out to the store at the last minute. I'd completely forgotten the ground ginger."

"Ground ginger," Trina repeated dubiously.

"What are you doing back from your father's so early?" Mrs. Sandburg asked. She took the flowers from the bag, filled a vase with water, and began arranging them.

"I thought you might need some help getting this dinner together."

Her mother faked an insulted expression. "Didn't you think I could manage to cook a fancy dinner on my own?"

Trina grinned. She gazed pointedly at the strange ingredients on the counter. "Exactly what kind of fancy dinner are you planning?"

"It's something I found in a magazine," Mrs. Sandburg said excitedly. "Mango chicken. It's a specialty of India. Look, here's the recipe."

Trina studied the description in the magazine. The instructions took up a whole page.

She spoke carefully. "This sounds awfully complicated, Mom. A little risky, if you know what I mean."

A crease of anxiety appeared on her mother's forehead. "Do you think so?"

Trina nodded. "Even a really experienced cook might have some trouble with this. And let's face it, Mom. You've got a lot of wonderful talents. But cooking . . . well, that's really not your specialty, is it?"

Her mother didn't appear to be the least bit offended, probably because Trina was speaking the truth. But still, she eyed the recipe wistfully. "This sounds so exotic and unusual, though. I thought it might really impress our guests."

Trina gave her mother a sympathetic smile. "I'll bet Dr. Fine and Sarah would be just as happy with something more ordinary that tastes good."

"Like what?" Mrs. Sandburg asked helplessly.

"How about plain old fried chicken? Everyone likes that."

"Maybe you're right," her mother said reluctantly. "You don't think Martin would find that boring, do you?"

Privately, Trina thought she would rather let her guests get bored than sick. "Fried chicken's never boring. And we'll have mashed potatoes with it, and a big green salad."

"I bought a nice, fresh, crunchy french bread," Mrs. Sandburg told her. "Now, I was thinking of making a chocolate mousse for dessert . . ."

Trina gulped. The last time her mother had attempted chocolate mousse it became chocolate soup.

"But I was afraid I wouldn't have enough time," Mrs. Sandburg continued. "So I picked up a cake at the bakery."

Trina breathed a sigh of relief. "Excellent. Now, let's put this stuff away and get started."

With only a small sigh of regret, her mother put away the yogurt and the mango and the fancy spices.

An hour later, the potatoes were peeled, cut up, and merrily boiling away in a pot. The lettuce and the other vegetables had been washed and cut up for a salad. Trina mixed an oil and vinegar dressing which she set aside to put on the salad at the last minute, so it wouldn't get soggy. The chicken had been cut up and floured, so it was all ready for frying.

"I'll set the table," Trina offered. "You can go get dressed."

Mrs. Sandburg hugged her. "You're a doll. Let's use the good china, okay?"

Her mother disappeared, and Trina pulled out the good china. They hardly ever used it, except for holidays and birthdays. She decided to use cloth napkins instead of paper, and she managed to locate some pretty napkin rings to put around them.

When she finished laying the table, she surveyed it with pride. It looked beautiful, especially with the flowers in the center.

But there was something missing, something that would add a certain mood to the table. She searched through drawers and found some candles.

She heard her mother behind her. "Trina, this looks lovely!"

"Thanks, Mom." She turned around. "I decided to—" She stopped when she got a good look at her mother. Mrs. Sandburg was always pretty. But tonight she looked downright glamorous. Her hair was arranged in soft curls around her face. A little makeup made her eyes look large and luminous. And the silk dress struck just the right note of elegance.

"Is that new?" Trina asked in wonder. Her mother hardly ever bought herself new clothes.

Mrs. Sandburg nodded. "Do you like it?"

"It's gorgeous!" Trina glanced down at her own jeans. "Um, I'll be right back."

She went to her room. She had planned to stay in her jeans for dinner. But this was beginning to look like a special evening, and she wanted to look the part. Rummaging through her closet, she picked out a simple, tailored navy blue wool dress and matching flats.

When she returned, her mother was going through their record albums. "What are you doing?" Trina asked.

"Picking out music."

Trina took one of her mother's favorite Rolling Stones albums. "How about this?"

"I don't think that would create the right mood. Here, let's try this one."

It was a record of classic waltzes. Mrs. Sandburg put it on the stereo. Seconds later, soft, flowing music with lots of violins filled the room. It was the kind of music Trina's friend Katie back at Sunnyside would call mushy. It was certainly romantic.

Yes, this was definitely going to be a special evening.

* * *

All dressed and ready to leave, Sarah paused for a minute at her desk to add a few lines to her letter to Alison. *Tonight we're having dinner at the Sandburgs'. All day Dad's been acting truly bizarre. One minute he's cracking dumb jokes and the next minute he's biting his fingernails! Trina told me her mother's not a great cook. But I don't think that's what is making him so nervous.*

Her father's voice boomed from downstairs. "Sarah! Let's go!"

Sarah left the letter on the desk. She had a feeling she'd have something more important to add later.

When she got downstairs and saw her father, she tried to keep her surprise from showing. But a little of it must have come through.

"Do you like it?" Dr. Fine asked.

"You're wearing a new suit!" Sarah exclaimed. "And it looks expensive!"

"It was," her father replied. "It's one of those fancy Italian designer suits."

Sarah had never seen her father look so handsome. Coming closer, she got a whiff of something. "And you're wearing cologne!"

24

"I didn't overdo it, did I?" he asked anxiously.

Sarah laughed. "You smell great, Dad. Let's go."

The ride to the Sandburgs' was quiet. Dr. Fine seemed preoccupied, lost in his own thoughts. That didn't bother Sarah. She was doing some thinking of her own. She was feeling a lot more excited than she'd normally be feeling, just going to a friend's for dinner. Something kept telling her that this was going to be an important evening.

When they arrived at the Sandburgs', they took the elevator up to the third floor. The minute they knocked, Mrs. Sandburg opened the door. "Welcome," she said warmly. "Come on in."

"Thank you," Dr. Fine said. He edged toward her, and then stopped. Sarah suspected that if *she* hadn't been standing right there, he would have gone even closer to Mrs. Sandburg.

"Where's Trina?" Sarah asked.

"In the kitchen," Mrs. Sandburg told her. "She's decided to take over dinner preparations."

"I'll go see if she needs any help," Sarah said.

25

Trina was pouring oil in a frying pan when Sarah entered. "Hi!"

"Hi," Sarah replied. "Mmm, fried chicken."

"How have you been?" Trina asked.

"Fine. How are you?"

"Fine."

"You look very nice," Sarah said.

"Thank you. So do you."

"Thank you."

Why were they talking like this? Sarah wondered. They'd known each other for four years. And here they were being so terribly polite, like people who barely knew each other.

"Have you heard from any of the cabin six girls lately?" Sarah asked.

"I get a letter from Katie every now and then. But she's not much of a writer."

"I got a postcard from Megan," Sarah said. "You never hear from Erin, do you?"

Trina shook her head. "I guess her social life keeps her too busy to write."

"Remember when we were at the ski resort, and she fell on the slopes?"

Trina grinned. "And she pretended she couldn't walk so she could get us to wait on her."

26

"It was a good thing they had that dance," Sarah said. "Otherwise, we'd never have gotten her out of that wheelchair!"

The memory made them both giggle, and that broke some of the tension. From the other room, they could hear their parents speaking in low voices, too quietly for them to hear the words.

"Something's going on in there," Sarah said.

"I know," Trina replied.

The gazed at each other in silence for a minute. "Trina," Sarah began slowly, "remember when they were both visiting Camp Sunnyside, and they started spending all that time together?"

Trina nodded. "And we were so afraid something romantic was going on between them."

"Yeah." Sarah hesitated, and then she smiled. "I'm not afraid anymore."

Trina smiled back. "Me neither." She dropped a piece of chicken into the sizzling oil.

"Trina! Sarah!" Mrs. Sandburg called. "Could you come in here?"

The girls hurried into the living room. Mrs. Sandburg and Dr. Fine were sitting side by side on the sofa. They were holding hands, and they weren't even trying to hide that. Sarah wasn't sure if their smiles were happy or nervous or a combination of both.

Dr. Fine turned to Mrs. Sandburg. "Would you like to tell them?"

"No, you tell them," she replied.

"Maybe you'd like to tell your daughter and I'll tell mine," he suggested.

"Or the other way around," she considered.

Sarah and Trina exchanged looks. "Why don't we tell you?" Sarah asked.

They both stared at the girls. "Tell us what?"

"You're getting married!" Trina burst out.

Their parents' mouths fell open. "How—how did you know?" Dr. Fine asked.

Both of the girls started laughing. As their parents recovered from the shock, they laughed too. "I hope this means you're both happy about this," Mrs. Sandburg said.

In response, Sarah hugged her father, and Trina hugged her mother. After releasing them, they stood there uncertainly for a second. Then Mrs. Sandburg held out her arms to Sarah. And Trina went into Dr. Fine's arms.

By now, Mrs. Sandburg and the girls were all squealing and giggling. Sarah was hopping up and down. A tear of joy ran down Mrs. Sandburg's face.

"When are you going to get married?" Trina asked.

At the same time, Sarah asked, "Where are we going to live?"

"Listen to our plans," Mrs. Sandburg began.

"Of course, they're subject to your approval," Dr. Fine added quickly. "We've decided that since we'll be a brand-new family, we need a brand-new place to live. So we're going to buy ourselves a new home."

For a second, Sarah felt a fleeting wave of regret at the thought of leaving the home she knew and loved. But it was a small price to pay for something so wonderful. Besides, she could always make her new bedroom look just like the one she was leaving.

"Then we'll be changing schools," Trina noted. She bit her lower lip. "In the middle of the year."

"We've got that all figured out," Mrs. Sandburg said. "We'll buy a house in Glenwood. That's halfway between where both families live now. That way, you girls can finish up the sixth grade at your own schools. Then, in the fall, you can both start Glenwood Middle School together."

29

"Sounds good to me," Sarah said.

Trina agreed. "After all, we would have been starting at new middle schools anyway."

"But you still haven't told us when you're getting married," Sarah pointed out.

"How does February fourteenth sound to you?" Dr. Fine asked.

"That's Valentine's Day!" Trina squealed. "How romantic!"

"Perfect!" Sarah echoed.

Dr. Fine looked at Trina. "Trina, I know you already have a father who you love very much. I don't expect to take his place. But I hope you'll be able to think of me as dad number two."

Mrs. Sandburg's face became serious as she turned to Sarah. "Sarah, dear, your father says you don't remember your own mother. I hope you'll be able to think of me as a real mother."

Sarah felt a surge of warmth rush through her. Looking at Trina, she saw the same feelings in her face.

"And how will you two feel about being sisters?" Dr. Fine asked.

Trina grinned. "It's not like we're total strangers. After all, we've been cabin mates for four years."

"Yeah," Sarah said. "Cabin mates, sisters—what's the difference?"

"And I know Alison from when she was a counselor at Sunnyside," Trina added.

"Dad," Sarah said, "let's call Alison right now and tell her the news."

But before he moved, Dr. Fine sniffed. "I smell something strange."

"Ohmigosh!" Trina wailed. "The chicken!" She ran back to the kitchen, and Sarah followed. Behind them, they heard their parents laughing.

"How about if I take over the cooking in this new family?" Dr. Fine suggested.

What a day. Trina was exhausted. But still, she had to take a few minutes to note this special day in her diary. She wrote:

Dear Diary, Something wonderful has happened. Mom and Dr. Fine are getting married on Valentine's Day. Sarah and I are going to be bridesmaids! We're going to move to a new house. I still can't believe this is happening— it's almost too good to be true. Mom won't be lonely anymore. I'm very happy for her, and

31

I'm happy for me, too. I won't be an only child anymore.

I've read books and seen TV shows where people get married and the two families don't get along. That won't happen to us!

Everything is going to be perfect.

Chapter 3

A week later, sitting in the backseat of the car, Sarah leaned forward as she spotted the big road sign that read WELCOME TO GLENWOOD.

"Is this the street?" she asked.

On the other side of the seat, Trina had her face pressed against the window. "Are we getting close?"

Dr. Fine slowed the car and paused in front of a dilapidated cottage. What little paint was left on it was peeling, and the windows were broken. "Well, girls, what do you think?"

Sarah stared at the ramshackle house in disbelief, and her stomach turned over. She knew her father enjoyed fixing things up, but this was ridiculous. Beside her, Trina's expression reflected the same dismay. But in her typical look-on-the-bright-side way, she managed to stammer, "It's . . . it's got a big yard."

From the passenger seat up front, Mrs. Sandburg laughed. "Martin, don't tease them. This isn't the house, girls."

Trina and Sarah uttered sighs of relief in unison. Dr. Fine chuckled. "I just figured that if they saw this one first, the one we like will look even better to them."

Mrs. Sandburg turned around and faced the girls. "But remember, girls, this is going to be your decision too. We haven't signed a contract or paid any money yet. We want you to be happy with your new home. If you don't like the one we're going to show you, we'll just keep looking."

Sarah nodded in appreciation. She knew that Mrs. Sandburg meant what she was saying. Mentally, she corrected herself. Not Mrs. Sandburg—Laura. That's what she was supposed to call her from now on. And Trina would be calling Sarah's father Martin.

It would feel a little odd calling a grown-up by her first name. But Laura wasn't just any grown-up. She was about to be Sarah's stepmother.

Stepmother. What a weird word. It brought back instant memories of all those fairy tales Sarah had read as a child. It was never just

34

"stepmother," it was always "wicked step-mother." The two words seemed to go together naturally.

And that was silly. By now, Sarah had been around Laura long enough to know that Laura could never be wicked. Someone should come up with a better word for the woman who married a person's father.

Dr. Fine turned to the left, then to the right. They were passing some nice-looking houses now. Sarah knew there was no point in being impatient, but she couldn't resist. "Are we almost there?"

"It's the next right," her father told her.

Sarah watched for the street sign as her father turned. Marigold Lane. She liked the sound of it.

"Here we are," Laura announced.

"No joking this time," Dr. Fine added. He pulled the car up to the curb and turned off the engine.

"Oh, wow," Trina breathed.

"No kidding," Sarah agreed fervently. They both jumped out of the car to get a better look.

It was a two-story house, not too old but not modern either. Set way back from the road, it was a gleaming white, with dark green shutters around the windows. Steps led up to a big porch. On the porch, there was an old-fashioned swing.

"Does the swing come with the house?" Trina asked.

Dr. Fine grinned. "I think that's negotiable. Well, how about a look inside?"

Trina and Sarah raced up the cobblestone walk ahead of their parents and climbed the stairs. Sarah jiggled the doorknob.

"It's locked, Dad."

"There's a note taped to the door," Trina said.

Mrs. Sandburg joined them and read it. Then she turned to Dr. Fine. "We have to pick up the keys at the realtors."

"That's just a few blocks away," Dr. Fine said. "C'mon, folks."

"Can we wait here and sit on the swing?" Trina asked suddenly.

"I suppose that will be okay," Mrs. Sandburg said. "We'll be right back."

The adults headed back to the car, and the girls settled themselves on the swing. For a few seconds, they swayed back and forth in silence. It was cold, but the girls were bundled up in heavy jackets and the sun was shining.

Then Trina spoke. "This is the first time

we've had a chance to talk by ourselves since—
you know."

Sarah nodded. "Yeah. How do you feel about
all this?"

"Good," Trina replied. "I really like your father."

"I like your mother too," Sarah said.

"And we like each other," Trina continued.
"So I don't think there are going to be any problems, do you?"

"Not a bit," Sarah stated. "Of course, it's going to be different, living together."

"But we've done that at Sunnyside," Trina
pointed out.

"That's true." Sarah shivered a little, but not
from the cold. "Wow, Trina. We're going to be
sisters. Well, stepsisters, really."

Trina made a face. "I don't like that word. It
sounds like Cinderella. Let's just say sisters."

"Sounds good to me," Sarah replied happily.

"I think we're very lucky," Trina said. "I
knew this girl at school whose father got married last year. She didn't get along with her new
stepsister. She told us the most awful stories
about her."

"Were they the same age?" Sarah asked.

"No, the stepsister was a year older. They

fought all the time, about everything. Like, whose turn it was to do the dishes, that sort of thing."

"Did they ever start getting along?" Sarah asked.

Trina shook her head. She was silent for a minute. Then, in a low voice, she said, "Their parents were getting divorced."

Sarah shuddered. "How awful! Well, our family will never be like that."

"Never," Trina agreed. "We're going to be one, big, happy family."

"We *have* to be," Sarah said. "You know, if our parents thought for one second that you and I wouldn't get along, they might not get married. It's very important to them that you and I be just as happy about all this as they are."

"You're right," Trina said. "I heard them talking about it at our apartment one night when they thought I was asleep. My mother was saying she was afraid that I'd have a hard time getting used to having sisters, because I've always been an only child. Of course, she's wrong," she added hastily.

Sarah believed her. Back at camp, Trina always said she envied the girls who had brothers and sisters. "Of course, there might be times when we don't agree about everything," she warned Trina. "I mean, Alison and I . . . well, we don't really fight very much, but we're not always on the same side, if you know what I mean."

Trina frowned slightly. "It's okay for you and Alison. But you know our parents will be watching us for any signs that we don't get along."

Sarah considered this. "You're right. Remember last Sunday, when my father had to work at the hospital and your mother took us to the movies? And we both wanted to see different movies?"

Trina nodded. "My mother looked so worried, like she was afraid we'd get into a big fight over it."

"Yeah." Sarah looked at Trina seriously. "We're going to have to be very careful."

Trina agreed. "We have to make sure they know we're happy together. Even if we disagree about something, we can't let it show. We don't want to risk ruining this for them."

Sarah had an idea. Maybe it was a little silly, but it seemed right. "Remember at Sunnyside, when we used to make pledges? Let's do that now."

She was pleased that Trina immediately agreed. "Okay. You want to start?"

Sarah raised her right hand. "We vow to always be loving sisters and never fight."

Trina raised her hand. "And we'll never do or say anything that might make our parents think we're not getting along." Then, in the Camp Sunnyside tradition, they slapped their palms together.

They finished their vow just in time. Dr. Fine's car pulled up, and their parents got out.

"We love this swing," Trina said as the adults approached.

"Let's hope the rest of the house meets with your approval," her mother said. Dr. Fine opened the front door, and they all went in.

They found themselves in a spacious foyer. Mrs. Sandburg led the tour of the empty house, describing each room. "Here's the living room. Isn't the fireplace pretty? And this could be the den, where we can put the TV. The kitchen is here."

Dr. Fine smiled hugely as he pointed out all the modern appliances and the huge counter space. "I could have some fun in here," he said, rubbing his hands in glee.

Sarah giggled. "Dad loves to spread things out

all over the place when he cooks. The food's great, but he makes the most unbelievable mess!"

"That's okay," Trina said. "He'll have us to clean up after him. Right?"

"Absolutely!" Sarah said quickly. Her father gave her a quizzical look. He was probably thinking of all the times Sarah fussed and complained about cleaning up. Well, there'd be no fussing or complaining in *this* house, she thought.

Upstairs, Mrs. Sandburg pointed out the master bedroom. "And it has its own bathroom," she said.

Sarah and Trina averted their eyes. Sarah knew Trina was feeling the same way she felt— a little uncomfortable at the thought of their parents sharing the same bedroom and bathroom. But she knew they'd get used to the idea.

"There are three more bedrooms," Mrs. Sandburg went on. "One for each of you, and one for Alison."

"Of course, now that Alison's away at college, she won't be here that much," Dr. Fine added. "So we can use her room as a guest room too."

"Wait a minute, Mom," Trina said. "Where are you going to write?"

"Oh, I can use the den, or work in the bedroom."

Trina looked concerned. "But you're used to having an office."

Sarah hesitated. Here was a perfect opportunity to show them how well the two girls got along. "I've got an idea. Trina and I could share a bedroom. And Mrs.—I mean, Laura, could use the other bedroom for an office."

"But don't you girls want your own rooms?" Dr. Fine asked.

"We'd *like* to share," Trina said quickly. "It would be fun, wouldn't it, Sarah?"

"Absolutely!"

Mrs. Sandburg looked doubtful, but Dr. Fine beamed. He turned to Mrs. Sandburg. "It sounds to me like we've got two girls who really want to be sisters."

"You got it!" Sarah said.

"But you've each got your own furniture," Mrs. Sandburg pointed out. "And I don't think the bedroom's big enough for all of it."

"We'll let them redecorate!" Dr. Fine suggested. "Brand-new furniture for brand-new sisters. How does that sound, girls?"

"Super!" they exclaimed in unison.

Later that afternoon, back at her old house,

Sarah looked around her bedroom. She'd had this furniture for a long time. Of course, it was nothing special. That lamp by her bed was sort of babyish. And her old desk was scratched and chipped.

Still, she found herself stroking the worn edge of the desk as she sat down and pulled out a piece of stationery.

Dear Megan, she wrote. *You're invited to a wedding! No, not mine, silly. My father and Trina's mother are getting married! On Valentine's Day! Isn't that romantic? Trina and I are really excited. We're going to be bridesmaids! Our parents told us we could invite all the cabin six girls to come to the wedding, and stay here for the weekend. The wedding's going to be at a hotel, and they're going to stay there for the weekend. But tell your parents that Alison will be here, to act like a counselor!*

Can you believe Trina and I are going to be sisters? She paused for a moment. Then she scrawled, *I still don't believe it myself.*

A few days later, Trina hurried home from school. "I'm home!" she called as she ran inside.

"All ready to go shopping for bridesmaid dresses?" her mother asked.

"Sure, just let me get rid of these books."

Mrs. Sandburg followed Trina into her bedroom. "Trina, are you sure you want to share a bedroom in the new house? You always liked your privacy."

"We want to, Mom. Really."

On the way to pick up Sarah, her mother chattered happily about the wedding plans. "It will be small, but elegant. Have you heard from your Sunnyside friends?"

"They're all coming," Trina said. "And boy, were they surprised to hear the news! Especially Erin. Back when you and Dr. Fine, I mean Martin, came to Sunnyside, Erin kept saying she thought something romantic was going on between the two of you."

"But nothing was going on," her mother said. "I was just interviewing him." She smiled. "I'm glad it happened that way. We were good friends before we fell in love."

"It's funny, in a way," Trina mused. "Back then, Sarah and I were so worried that Erin was right. But now we're happy!"

"I think we'll all make a good family," Mrs. Sandburg said.

"Better than good. We'll be the *perfect* family."

Her mother laughed. "Well, nobody's perfect."

"We'll be," Trina insisted.

Sarah was waiting for them in front of her house. From there, it was only a short drive to the mall.

"What kind of dresses are we going to get?" Sarah asked as they strolled through the mall and looked in windows.

"Usually bridesmaids wear identical dresses," Mrs. Sandburg said. "But you girls don't have to."

Trina couldn't imagine the same dress looking good on both her and Sarah. Trina was tall and lanky. Sarah was shorter and a little chubby.

But Sarah seemed to think otherwise. "I think it would look better if we got the same dress. More traditional. Ooh, look at that one!"

They paused before the window of a store called Junior Fantasies. The dress Sarah had her eyes on was pale pink, made out of some thin, gauzy material. It had an oversized lace collar and big, flowing sleeves that gathered at the wrists.

"It's pretty," Mrs. Sandburg said. "How do you like it, Trina?"

Objectively, Trina had to admit that it was a pretty dress. But it wasn't her style at all—too girlish, too frilly. "It's nice . . ." she began slowly.

"Can we try it on?" Sarah asked eagerly.

They went into the store, and asked a saleslady for assistance. She found the dress in both the girls' sizes, and they took them into the dressing room.

"Oh, I love it," Sarah exclaimed in rapture. She pirouetted in front of the mirror. "And it fits perfectly! Trina, what do you think?"

"You look adorable," Trina said honestly. The flowing lines made Sarah look thinner, and the pink color gave her cheeks a rosy glow.

Then she checked her own reflection. The dress fit—but that was about the best she could say about it. Pink wasn't her color. It made her look sallow. And the femininity of the dress seemed odd with her short, boyish hairdo.

Her mother stood behind them, watching them both thoughtfully. Trina tried to keep her face expressionless, but surely her mother could see that the dress wasn't right for her. She'd never say anything, though. Mrs. Sandburg always let Trina choose her own clothes. And since Trina's choices were usually pretty conservative, there was rarely anything to object to anyway.

Sarah was too caught up in her own image to notice Trina's lack of enthusiasm. "I hope it's not too expensive," she said. "Laura, wouldn't these be perfect for a wedding?"

"It certainly looks lovely on you, dear," Mrs. Sandburg said. "I think it's perfect for you. Of course, Trina may want something different."

Sarah's face fell. "I want us to dress alike. It will look so much nicer for the ceremony. Trina, if you don't like this one, we'll find something else we both like." But her wistful eyes kept drifting back to the mirror.

"Oh no, I like this one too," Trina said quickly.

"Are you sure?" her mother asked. Trina couldn't blame her for looking a little surprised. This dress wasn't Trina's taste at all.

"Yes, I think it would be nice for a change," Trina insisted. The delight in Sarah's eyes was enough to compensate.

Mrs. Sandburg checked the price tags. "These look like they're within our budget."

The girls changed back into their regular clothes, and Mrs. Sandburg paid for the dresses.

"Now we have to stop by the florists to order

47

my bouquet," Mrs. Sandburg said. "And yours too."

Trina's eyes lit up. She loved flowers. "We get bouquets too?"

"Whoever heard of a bridesmaid without a bouquet?" Mrs. Sandburg replied gaily.

The florist shop was heavenly. The girls wandered around, oohing and ahhing over all the different flowers and arrangements. Mrs. Sandburg ordered pink roses and baby's breath for herself. Trina spotted a selection of tiny white tea roses.

"Oh, Sarah, look at these!"

Sarah joined her. "They're nice." There was a definite lack of excitement in her voice. And her eyes kept drifting over to the lilacs.

The lilacs looked awfully big to Trina. Surely, the bridesmaids' bouquets shouldn't be bigger than the bride's.

"What have you girls picked out?" Mrs. Sandburg asked.

"We haven't really decided—" Trina began, but Sarah interrupted.

"We both love these tea roses."

Trina looked at her in surprise. "Are you sure?"

Sarah nodded firmly. "Absolutely. Let's order the tea roses."

"My, you two are awfully easy to please," Mrs. Sandburg commented. "You're agreeing about everything!"

"That's the kind of sisters we are," Sarah said. "Right Trina?"

"Right," Trina agreed. So what if she had to wear a dress she didn't like, and Sarah had to carry flowers she wasn't crazy about? The important thing was that her mother see that she and Sarah got along and didn't argue over every little thing.

So far, they were doing just fine.

Chapter 4

Dear Diary, Trina wrote. *Today is Friday, and this is the last entry I'll be writing while sitting at this desk. In fact, this is the last time I'll be writing in this room. But I don't feel the least bit sad about it.*

All my clothes and books and things are in boxes and suitcases. I'll be spending the weekend at Sarah's house. All the cabin six girls are coming there. They're probably there already, waiting for me. Tomorrow is the wedding. On Sunday, we move into the new house.

She paused. Just thinking about the next couple of days made her breathless. But she still had more to write.

Yesterday, we practiced the wedding ceremony. Then we shopped for new furniture for the bedroom Sarah and I will share. I saw some beautiful modern stuff I really liked. Sarah said it was okay too, but she kept looking at the more old-fashioned furniture. I hope she doesn't mind that we bought the modern furniture. I'm sure that once we get settled, everything's going to be fine.

Meanwhile, I'm excited about seeing Katie and Megan and Erin. And the wedding is going to be wonderful. I know that Mom and Dr. Fine—

quickly she crossed that out and wrote *Martin.* Was she ever going to get used to thinking of him like that?

I know that Mom and Martin are going to be just as happy together as Dad and Shelly are, as long as Sarah and I don't do anything to mess things up. And we won't.

She underlined those last three words twice. And she added an exclamation point.

"Trina? It's time to go." Mrs. Sandburg stood in the doorway.

"Okay." Trina closed her diary and stuck it in the suitcase that lay open on her bed. She caught a glimpse of her bridesmaid dress inside, and shuddered. Then she shut the suitcase.

She felt her mother's hand on her shoulder. "How do you feel?"

"Fine. Why?"

"Well, we're leaving this apartment, closing

51

the door on our old life . . . this is going to be a big change for us."

"But it's a change for something better, Mom." Trina looked around the room. "To tell the truth, I never much liked this apartment anyway."

Her mother smiled. "Confidentially, neither did I." Then, without warning, she put her arms around Trina and hugged her tightly. "You know I love you very much. And no matter what else changes, that never will."

"I know that, Mom." Tears sprung into her eyes. Gazing up at her mother, she saw that *her* eyes were wet too.

"Look at us, crying on the day before my wedding. Aren't we being silly?"

"My eyes aren't red, are they?" Trina asked. "I wouldn't want the girls to think I've been crying. Megan, especially."

"She's the one with the wild imagination, isn't she?"

"Yeah." Trina grinned. "She's probably already worked up some wild fantasy about Sarah and me. She'll imagine we're both miserable about this and don't want the wedding to happen. And if she tells Katie that, Katie will have already come up with schemes and plans to help Sarah and me break you two up!"

Mrs. Sandburg started laughing. Then she stopped. "But none of that is true, is it? You *are* happy?"

"Mom! How many times do I have to tell you? We're happy! Thrilled! Ecstatic!" She grabbed her suitcase, and continued as they headed toward the door. "We're delighted! We're excited! We're full of joy!"

And they giggled all the way to the car.

At Sarah's house, Megan's face was pressed against the window. "Here comes Trina now!"

Sarah ran to the foot of the stairs. "Alison! Trina's here!"

Her older sister hurried downstairs. She looked excited but flustered, and Sarah couldn't blame her. When Alison had left to return to college after Christmas, everything had been normal and ordinary. She'd come back to find her family getting ready to move to a new house, and she was about to get a new mother and another younger sister. But despite all the changes and confusion, she was just as thrilled as Sarah.

Erin joined Megan at the window, where Megan was flapping her hand at the approaching figure. "Honestly, Megan, can't you wait until she gets inside?"

Katie couldn't. She tore out the door and ran toward Trina.

"She's going to freeze!" Alison yelled.

Sure enough, Katie's teeth were chattering as she returned with her arm around Trina. The girls all gathered around for a communal hug.

"I'm so glad you all could come!" Trina exclaimed.

"Just think!" Megan squealed. "A Sunnyside wedding!"

Erin gazed at her reprovingly. "I hope you don't have any stupid ideas, like bursting into the camp song in the middle of the ceremony."

Sarah looked at Trina and they both cracked up at the notion.

"Let's see your bridesmaid dresses," Erin urged.

"You'll see them tomorrow," Trina said quickly.

"Alison, are you going to be a bridesmaid too?" Katie asked.

Alison struck a pose. "As the oldest, *I'm* the maid of honor. Listen, you guys, I have to go make some phone calls." Her eyes twinkled. "Besides, I'm sure you all have a lot to say to

each other that you don't want a former counselor to hear." She left the room, and the girls
settled down on the floor of the living room.

"This is so exciting." Megan sighed. "I've
never been to a wedding before."

"I have," Erin said importantly. "Once, I
went to a wedding that had five hundred guests.
There were eight bridesmaids and two flower
girls. Afterwards, there was an orchestra and
dancing."

"Ours isn't going to be like that," Sarah told
her.

"It's going to be small but elegant," Trina
said.

Katie's eyes darted back and forth between
them with interest. "What I can't believe is that
you two are going to be sisters."

"Stepsisters," Erin corrected her.

"We prefer the word 'sisters,' " Trina said.

"Yeah," Sarah agreed. "Like a real family."

Megan turned to Trina. "I guess that's going
to be really different for you. I mean, Sarah already knows what it's like to have a sister. But
you've never had one."

"I think having Trina for a sister is going to
be a lot different from having Alison for one,"

Sarah said. "Mainly because Trina and I are never going to fight."

Katie looked skeptical. "Well, you have to argue sometimes. It's only natural."

"Not in this family," Trina stated.

"But that's impossible!" Megan exclaimed. "Think of Sunnyside! We all argue once in a while."

"Sunnyside's a camp," Trina said. "This is a family."

Katie chortled. "Hey, if it's going to be anything like *my* family . . ." She left the sentence unfinished, and everyone knew what she meant. They'd all been to Katie's home for a Sunnyside reunion. Katie had older twin brothers, and there was always lots of squabbling going on.

"But we won't be like that," Sarah insisted. "Right, Trina?"

"Right."

Katie rolled her eyes. "Hey, come on, you guys. Remember back at Sunnyside when your parents first met? And you thought something romantic was going on? You two were constantly snapping at each other."

Sarah had a clear memory of that. It was the only time she could remember Trina ever getting really mean. "That's all in the past. We're happy about it now."

"We're moving into a new house Sunday, and we're getting all new bedroom furniture," Trina told them.

Megan was looking at Sarah. "What's the matter?"

"Huh?"

"You just got this funny expression on your face. Don't you like the new house?"

"Oh, no, I love it. Hey, enough about us. What's going on with you guys?"

While they talked, Sarah decided she'd better watch her expressions. It was the mention of the bedroom furniture that had made her frown.

That awful modern stuff—how could Trina like it? Especially the two matching desks, sleek and shiny and skinny. Sarah thought about her old, worn desk upstairs. How was she ever going to write her poems and stories on that plain-looking new desk with its sharp edges?

But Trina had seemed to like it so much in the furniture store. And their parents had been there with them. There was no way Sarah could let her objections show. So she'd just smiled and nodded while Trina gushed over the ugly furniture. It wasn't easy, but what else could she have done?

Erin was talking. "You know, if you guys are smart, you can get a lot out of this marriage."

"Of course we'll get a lot," Trina replied. "A whole new family."

"You can get more than that," Erin went on. "I have a friend at school whose mother got remarried. She liked her stepfather okay, but she acted all depressed about the marriage, like it was messing up her life. Her mother and stepfather went all out trying to make it up to her. She got anything she wanted—her own television, a stereo, and tons of clothes. All you have to do is make your parents feel guilty."

Sarah shook her head. "I'd never do anything like that to my father."

"And I wouldn't do that to my mother," Trina agreed. "Besides, we already have everything we want. Right, Sarah?"

"Right," Sarah replied. Except for a decent desk . . .

The next day, the girls got off the hotel elevator and started down the hall. "I don't understand," Megan said. "Why couldn't you just dress at home?"

"Because our dresses might have gotten wrinkled in the car," Trina told her. She was carrying hers, covered with dark plastic, on a hanger.

Alison checked the number on the key that the man at the reception desk had given her. "Here's the room." She unlocked the door and the girls went inside.

"Wow!" Katie cried out. "This is *fancy!*"

Trina agreed. It wasn't just any old hotel room. It was a huge suite, with beautiful furniture. "This is where the reception is going to be after the ceremony."

Even Erin was impressed. She stroked the velvet couch. "Where are your parents?"

"They're changing in another room," Sarah said. "They're going to be staying there tonight."

"Just one night?" Erin raised her eyebrows. "That doesn't sound like much of a honeymoon."

"Dad's got a lot of patients and he can't get away from the hospital right now," Sarah said.

"And Mom has a writing deadline," Trina added. "So they're going to wait until summer to have a real honeymoon."

Katie was exploring the suite, opening doors

and peering inside. "Hey, there are three bed-rooms!"

"We'd better start getting ready," Alison said. "I'll take this one." She disappeared into a bed-room.

Trina turned to Sarah. "We could dress to-gether in this room here."

Megan looked puzzled. "Why bother to share? You can each have your own room."

Trina knew she'd prefer that. She'd been hop-ing to get a few minutes alone with Katie. But she didn't want Sarah to think she didn't want to dress with her.

Sarah, too, looked uncertain. Luckily, Katie took over. "Megan, you go in that room with Sarah. I'll take this one with Trina. Erin, you can go back and forth and help out."

That seemed agreeable to everyone. Katie grabbed Trina's arm, pulled her into a bedroom, and shut the door. She put her hands on her hips and faced Trina squarely.

"Okay, now tell me the truth."

"Huh?"

"How do you *really* feel about all this?"

Trina looked her straight in the eye. "I feel great. I like Sarah's father, and Sarah likes my mother. My mother and Martin are going to be very happy together."

"But what about you and Sarah?"

Trina rolled her eyes. "Oh, Katie. You know I like Sarah! And it's not like we're strangers."

"But are you really going to share a bedroom at the new house?"

Trina nodded, and Katie grimaced. "I'd hate that. And I can't believe you're absolutely thrilled with that either. You've always had your own bedroom, and so has Sarah. I'm surprised your parents are making you share."

Trina bit her lower lip. "They're not making us do anything. It was *our* idea. So my mother could have one of the bedrooms as an office. It doesn't matter. Sarah and I get along. We can work it out."

Katie looked doubtful. "Hmm . . . well, let's see your bridesmaid dress."

Trina took the plastic off the hanger. Katie stared at the dress long and hard before speaking.

"Don't you like it?" Trina asked.

Katie spoke carefully. "I guess it's pretty. It just doesn't seem like your style. Who picked it?"

"We did."

Katie's eyes narrowed. "That doesn't look like a dress you'd choose."

"Well, Sarah actually picked the dresses," Trina admitted.

"Tell the truth," Katie demanded. "Do *you* like the dress?"

It was impossible to lie to Katie. Trina just smiled thinly and shrugged.

Katie's eyebrows shot up. "And you just went along with Sarah's choice?"

"I didn't want to start an argument."

"Good grief," Katie said. "Sarah's not that touchy. If you told her you weren't crazy about the dress, she wouldn't have minded. You could have found something else you both liked."

"But Sarah really loved it, I could tell. Besides, my mother was with us. We didn't want her to think that we might not get along. She and Dr. Fine are worried about that. If they thought we couldn't even agree on a dress, I'm afraid they might have ended up canceling the whole marriage! Besides, it's just a dress, no big deal."

"I guess you've got a point," Katie said. "Anyway, it's not *that* awful. Let's see how it looks on you."

Trina slipped out of her jeans and pulled on the dress. Katie circled her.

"Well, it fits. And you don't look *bad.*"

Trina grinned. "Thanks a lot for the compliment."

Erin walked in. "Okay, I'm finished with Sarah. Now I can get started on you." She examined Trina critically. "No offense, but that dress looks better on Sarah."

"I know, I know," Trina said wearily. "What do you think you're going to do with me, anyway?"

"Well, there's not much I can do about your hair. But I can put on your makeup."

"I don't wear makeup," Trina objected.

"Trina, it's your mother's wedding day! You *have* to wear makeup!"

"Gee, is that a new law I never heard of?" Katie deepened her voice. "It is hereby required that all girls shall wear makeup on their mothers' wedding days or suffer the consequences."

Trina giggled nervously, but Erin ignored Katie. She whipped a bag out of her purse, and began pulling out little compacts and tubes.

"Now, don't put too much on me," Trina cautioned.

63

"I know what I'm doing," Erin insisted. "Sit down."

"Don't let her make me look like a clown," Trina pleaded to Katie. She sat very still as Erin dipped little brushes into colored powders and swept them across her eyes and cheeks. She outlined Trina's lips with a pencil and filled them in with a pale pink lipstick.

"Now, look at yourself."

In the mirror, Trina could see Erin standing behind her, looking very proud. And Trina had to admit Erin deserved to feel proud. The makeup actually looked nice. Very subtle, but it added a glow to her sallow cheeks and made her eyes look larger.

"Now, let's go see Sarah," Katie said.

As they went back out into the main room, Sarah and Megan were emerging from the other bedroom.

"Sarah!" Trina cried out. "You look beautiful!"

"So do you!" Sarah replied.

Then Alison came out of her room. As maid of honor, her dress was different, more grown-up looking. But the deep rose color blended well with the pink dresses Sarah and Trina were wearing. With her hair up, Alison looked very sophisticated.

As the girls complimented her, there was a knock on the door. "Who is it?" Alison asked.

"Florist delivery."

Alison opened the door. "Here are the bouquets!" She passed the tea roses to Sarah and Trina, and took one for herself. A second later, there was another knock on the door. Katie opened it.

"Mom!" Trina gazed at her mother in wonderment. She'd always thought her mother was pretty. But she'd never seen her look like this. She could have been a movie star!

"Mrs. Sandburg, you're beautiful!" Katie breathed.

"Exquisite," Erin said.

Mrs. Sandburg smiled brightly. "Thank you, girls. I'm so glad you're here to share this with us."

"Just think," Megan murmured. "After this ceremony, we won't be able to call you Mrs. Sandburg anymore. You'll be Mrs. Fine."

Trina caught her breath. Of course, Megan was right. But it hadn't occurred to Trina before. After today, she and her mother wouldn't

65

be sharing the same last name. It gave her a strange feeling. But she didn't let it show.

"Let me look at my daughters," her mother said. Trina and Sarah and Alison stepped forward. Mrs. Sandburg's warm eyes swept over them. "I feel like the happiest, luckiest woman on earth today," she said simply. Then she looked at the clock. "Oh, my, look at the time."

"We'd better get downstairs if we want good seats," Katie said. "C'mon, you guys." She left with Megan and Erin.

Then Dr. Fine walked in.

"Hey, you're not supposed to see the bride before the wedding," Sarah objected. "It's bad luck."

Trina's mother laughed and stepped in back of him. "Okay, okay," Dr. Fine said. "But there's no superstition that says I can't look at my daughters. Wow, you three are beautiful. Am I a lucky fellow or what?"

"Martin, we'd better get going," Mrs. Sandburg murmured.

Together, they went down the hall to the elevator. All of them became silent as they rode down, lost in their own private thoughts.

At the entrance to the room where the ceremony was to be held, Dr. Fine took a deep breath and squared his shoulders. "Well, see you guys soon." He went through the double doors.

A moment later, they heard the organ music begin. Alison went through the doors first. Together, Trina and Sarah counted to five, the way they'd been taught at the rehearsal. Then, side by side, they walked in together.

They moved slowly down the aisle. Mentally, hoping her lips weren't moving, Trina counted the rhythm so they'd stay together. One, and two, and three . . .

Out of the corner of her eye, Trina could see the faces turned toward them. There were friends of her mother's, friends of Dr. Fine's, and people they worked with. Megan's red hair stood out. Katie was grinning. But Trina kept her eyes on the man in the robe behind a podium who stood at the end of the aisle.

When they reached the podium, the girls separated, Sarah going to the right of the podium and Trina to the left. Then they turned toward the doors.

The music became louder. The doors swung open. And there stood Trina's mother.

Even though she was a small woman, she came down the aisle like a queen. Trina could feel tears of joy welling in her eyes. She hoped they wouldn't trickle down and ruin Erin's careful makeup job.

When her mother reached the podium, she handed her bouquet to Alison. Then she and Dr. Fine joined hands.

The man in the robe spoke. "Friends, we are gathered here to witness this man and this woman as they join in marriage."

For Trina, the next few moments seemed hazy, like a dream. There were more words, lots of them, but they floated over Trina's head. The only ones that stood out were "I do," spoken twice. Dr. Fine placed a ring on her mother's finger, and she placed one on his. They kissed.

And then it was over. The couple made their way back up the aisle. Alison followed them. Together, Trina and Sarah followed Alison.

Once outside the room, both parents opened their arms and the girls fell into them.

"I'd like to stay in this position for another hour," Trina's mother murmured. "But we'd better get up to the reception before the guests get there."

They moved toward the elevators. Sarah and Trina lagged slightly behind. Sarah turned to Trina with a huge smile.

"Hiya, sis."

"Hiya, sis."

Oh yes, Trina thought happily. Everything is going to be absolutely perfect.

Chapter 5

A little over a week later, as she rode the bus home from school, Sarah reflected on her new family, her new home, her new life. So far, so good, she thought. Some parts of her new life were major improvements over her old life.

Like Laura, for example. Despite the fact that Sarah had liked her before the marriage, she had been a little worried about what it would be like to actually live with a stepmother. Would she have to start behaving and doing things differently from before? Would Laura start ordering her around, telling her what to do and how to do it?

That hadn't turned out to be the case at all. Laura was truly fantastic. Since Sarah couldn't remember her own mother, she wasn't quite sure what to expect from her. All she knew about mothers came from her experiences with friends' families, books, and television. Some of the mother-and-daughter relationships she'd seen weren't all that great.

But Sarah felt totally comfortable with Laura. They had lots in common—a love of books and writing, for example. It was so nice having her around. She was smart, and good-natured, and easygoing. Sarah felt as if she could talk to her about anything and everything. And it was amazing how she'd changed her father! He used to be so serious and quiet. Now, he seemed much more relaxed and cheerful.

She gazed out the bus window. She liked Glenwood better than her old neighborhood. It was much friendlier. During the past week, neighbors had come by to say hello and welcome. She hadn't been to the local public library yet, but she'd seen it, and it looked bigger than the one back in her old town.

The only drawback was the fact that she couldn't walk to her old school anymore. But that was working out okay. Their next-door neighbor had a job near Sarah's school, and she dropped her off every morning. Her father dropped Trina off at her school on the way to the hospital. They both took buses home.

For the first couple of days after the wedding,

things had been a little crazy and confused. The Sunnyside girls had left, Alison had gone back to college, and they'd moved into the new house. They'd settled in quickly, and now they were in a comfortable, regular routine.

Sarah got off the bus, which stopped only a block from the house. As she hurried toward it, she decided that the new house was beginning to feel like home. At least, most of it did—the living room, the den, the kitchen, the dining room. There was only one room that didn't feel right yet.

Unfortunately, it was the most important room in the house to her.

But maybe what she was bringing home today would help make her feel better about it. She hurried up the walk to the house, went inside, and ran up the stairs.

Trina was already in the bedroom. She was lying on her bed, writing in a little notebook, which she closed the second Sarah entered.

"Hi! Where have you been?"

"I stayed late at school," Sarah replied. "There was a fair in the gym, some sort of fundraising deal the PTA was having. Wait till you see what I got!"

She dumped the three rolled tubes of paper

on her own bed. Trina got up and came over. "What are they?"

"Posters! For our walls." Sarah started unrolling them. They were the biggest posters she had ever seen. She'd chosen them for that very reason. The bigger the posters, the more of the walls they'd cover.

She hadn't said a word when Trina suggested the tan paint for their bedroom walls. She couldn't, because their parents had been with them in the paint store. So she had faked delight at Trina's choice, and had gone along with it. Their parents had seemed very pleased that the decision was made so easily, and Sarah was glad she hadn't objected.

But every time Sarah looked at the dull, dreary walls, she felt a little down, and found herself missing the bright pink walls of the bedroom she had left.

These posters would help, she thought. All three were wild, abstract designs with bright colors. Laying them out flat on the bed, she turned to Trina expectantly. "Cool, huh?"

Gazing at the posters, Trina seemed to be momentarily speechless. Then she said, "Yeah, they're great."

"Let's put them up right away," Sarah suggested. "Have you got any tape?"

"Yes." Trina went to her desk and opened a drawer. Sarah looked in amazement at how neat everything was inside. The inside of her own desk drawer was a jumble of stuff.

Even with the drawers closed, it was hard to believe these were identical desks. Trina's desk top was organized—notebooks gathered in a precise pile, schoolbooks stacked to the side, pens and pencils in a little round holder, and a calendar perfectly centered in the middle.

Sarah's desk top, on the other hand, couldn't even be seen with everything haphazardly tossed on it.

Sarah took Trina's desk chair and pulled it toward the wall. "What are you doing?" Trina asked.

"I'll have to stand on this to put the posters up."

"With your shoes on?"

"Huh?" Sarah looked at her blankly.

"Never mind," Trina said hastily. "Let me do it. I'm taller." She took off her shoes, and climbed up on the chair. Sarah handed her the posters one by one.

"Does this look even?" Trina asked, holding the first poster against the wall.

"Looks fine to me," Sarah said.

Trina applied some tape, got off the chair, and examined it. "I think it's about a quarter of an inch low on the left," she murmured. She got back up on the chair and adjusted it.

Who cared about a quarter of an inch? Sarah wondered. Trina fussed like that over each of the posters. Finally, they were all up.

"Wow, what an improvement!" Sarah exclaimed.

Trina got down off the chair, stepped back, and looked. "Yes, they're very nice."

Sarah went over to her bed. Then she frowned. "Where is it?" she muttered to herself.

"What's the matter?" Trina asked.

"I can't find my book. The one I was reading last night. I know I left it here."

"I put it in the bookshelf," Trina told her.

"Why?"

"That's where books belong, right?"

Sarah smiled thinly. "Right." Trina had a point. But Sarah always liked to find things right where she'd left them. It took her a while, searching the bookcase, to find the book.

Trina was at her desk. "This is weird. My colored marking pens aren't where I always put them."

"Oh, I borrowed them last night," Sarah said. She went to her own desk, and searched through the piles of papers and books and assorted junk that was sitting on top. "I was making a cover for a report I had to turn in. Here they are. You don't mind that I borrowed them, do you?"

There was just the slightest hesitation before Trina said, "Of course not."

"Sarah! Trina!"

The girls went out to the hall. Laura stood at the bottom of the stairs.

"I just talked to Martin," she said. "He's got an emergency at the hospital, so he won't be home for dinner. And I just didn't have time today to get to the supermarket. So I thought I'd run out and pick up some take-out food for us. What would you girls like?"

"What are the choices?" Sarah asked.

"Well, let's see. I noticed a bunch of take-out places over on the highway. There's pizza, fried chicken, burgers, tacos, Chinese food . . ."

"Tacos!" Sarah said.

At the very same instant, Trina called, "Pizza!" Then they both stared at each other.

"Actually, pizza sounds good," Sarah said quickly.

"No, I've changed my mind," Trina stated. "I'm in the mood for tacos too."

Laura laughed. "My, you guys are polite! Would you like to flip a coin?"

Trina turned to Sarah. "You choose. I'll go along with anything you want."

"No, really, I can eat anything," Sarah insisted. "Laura, what do you like best?"

"Well, personally, I prefer Chinese food. But—"

"Chinese food is great," Sarah interrupted.

"I think so too," Trina said.

"Are you sure?" Mrs. Sandburg asked. Both girls nodded, and she took her coat from the coatrack in the foyer. "Okay, I'll go now."

After she left, Sarah turned to Trina. "Did you get much homework today?"

"I managed to do it all during library time at school," Trina said. "What about you?"

Sarah was amazed. When her class had library time, she always spent the time reading for pleasure, not doing homework. "I just have to come up with an essay topic. Want to play Monopoly or something?"

"It's my turn to set the table. I'd better go do it now so we'll be ready to eat when my mother gets back."

Sarah herself would have waited till the last minute.

"We can play a game after dinner," Trina suggested.

"Sure, that'll be fine," Sarah agreed.

Sarah went back to the bedroom. Actually, she was sort of glad Trina hadn't wanted to play a game right then. It was nice to have a few minutes alone, and she wanted to take advantage of it. She went to her desk, pulled out a sheet of stationery, and started a letter to Megan.

Dear Megan, she wrote. *It was great having you here for the wedding. We're all moved in and settled now. Everything's going fine here.*

She spent a few minutes describing their neighbors, and how much she liked having Laura for a stepmother. There was something else she wanted to write about too, but she felt a little odd about it. Still, it always made her feel better when she put her thoughts on paper.

It's funny, though. I never realized before how different Trina and I are. She's so tidy and or-

ganized. Not that I'm a slob. Okay, maybe I am, a little. But Trina's the complete opposite!

Of course, that's not important. We're getting along perfectly.

The sound of footsteps made her turn around. Trina was back. Sarah pushed the letter aside.

Later, that evening, Trina stretched out on her bed, closed her eyes, and lay very still. All she wanted to do right that minute was enjoy the silence of the room. Sarah was down in the kitchen, talking to Trina's mother about a topic for a school essay. How nice it was to be alone for a change!

Immediately, she felt guilty for even having such unfriendly thoughts. She opened her eyes and sat up. Then she wanted to close her eyes again.

Those awful posters! They absolutely ruined the room. And they practically covered the walls. There was no way to avoid looking at them. The thought of waking up every morning and seeing these ugly pictures made her feel slightly ill.

But there was nothing she could do about them. Sarah obviously loved them. Posters certainly weren't worth starting an argument over. Everything was going so well, and she wasn't about to risk messing up her family.

Of course, she wasn't silly enough to think a disagreement over posters could break up a marriage. But one argument could lead to another, and another. If she and Sarah weren't able to get along ... She shuddered at the thought of what their parents might do.

But Sarah really shouldn't have borrowed her marking pens without asking, either. Trina reached over to her nightstand and picked up her diary. It was time to get some of these bad feelings out.

She didn't have time to write anything more than "Dear Diary" before Sarah appeared at the door. Quickly, she shut the notebook and put it back.

"It's almost nine o'clock," Sarah announced.

"What happens at nine o'clock?" Trina asked.

"That's when *The Cooper Clan* comes on! Don't you watch it? It's my all-time number-one favorite TV show! C'mon, let's go down to the den."

Trina really wasn't in the mood to watch TV. But if she stayed in this room while Sarah was in the den, her mother might think something was wrong. She knew it would please their parents to see her and Sarah enjoying something together. "Okay," she said, and got off the bed.

"I can't believe you don't watch it," Sarah said as they went down the stairs. "It's so funny."

Trina didn't mention that she *had* seen *The Cooper Clan* before. Personally, she thought it was dumb. She hoped that just because Sarah liked it and watched it every week, she wouldn't have to start watching it too. And pretending to enjoy it.

In the den, Sarah turned on the TV, and the girls settled on the rug. Laura came in.

"What are you watching?"

"The Cooper Clan," Sarah told her. "It's a great show. Want to watch it with us?"

"All right," Laura said. "Trina, I don't remember you watching this before."

"I guess I never knew it was so good," Trina lied.

They heard the front door open, and a second later Martin came into the den. The girls greeted him, and Laura got up and planted a kiss on his cheek.

"Honey, you look tired," she said.

"I was," he admitted. "But I'm starting to pick up already. It's wonderful to come home and find my family all gathered together."

"Do you want something to eat?" Laura asked.

"No, I grabbed a bite in the hospital cafeteria." He joined Laura on the couch. "What are we about to watch?"

"One of Sarah's favorite TV shows," Laura told him. "What did you say it's called, Sarah?"

"*The Cooper Clan.* It's funny."

"Well, after my day, I could use a few laughs," Martin said. "Is this one of your favorite shows too, Trina?"

"I'm sure it *will* be," Trina said.

The show began, and Trina concentrated, determined to enjoy it.

It wasn't easy. *The Cooper Clan* was about a zany family who always found themselves in some silly situation. In this particular episode, the kids in the family were planning a surprise anniversary party for their parents. They were all so worried that they'd accidentally give away the secret that they avoided being around their parents. Meanwhile, the parents thought they weren't spending enough time together as a family, and kept planning get-togethers that the kids made excuses to get out of doing.

In the end, of course, they all realized what was going on, and everyone was happy. Trina thought the whole thing was stupid. But Sarah was cracking up. Their parents were talking softly together, and barely watching. But each time Sarah laughed, Trina forced herself to utter a feeble "ha-ha."

As soon as the show was over, Trina got up. She knew Sarah would want to talk about it, and Trina wasn't very good at lying. "I'm going to take a shower now," she announced.

At least the shower was one place where she could be alone. But she wondered if she would ever get used to taking her showers at night. She'd always been a morning shower taker. But so was Sarah. And there was never enough time in the morning for them both to use it.

Standing under the water, she thought about the show she'd just seen. One part of it that she had actually liked was the way the brothers and sisters in the family bickered and argued. She guessed real siblings could do that sort of thing. Like Katie and her brothers.

She stepped out of the shower, dried off, and put on her nightgown. She hoped Sarah was still

downstairs, watching television. She was looking forward to writing in her diary.

But when she went back into the bedroom,
Sarah was lying in bed, reading. And Trina just
didn't feel comfortable writing in her diary in
front of her.

It didn't really matter. She was pretty sleepy,
and she crawled into bed.

"Do you mind if I turn off the overhead light?"
she asked Sarah.

"No, go ahead. I'll use this one." Sarah
switched on the lamp by her bed.

Trina gazed at it in dismay. It was impossible
for her to sleep with any kind of light on at all.
But what could she do? She couldn't very well
ask Sarah to find a flashlight and read under
the covers, the way she did at Sunnyside.

There was a rap on the door. "Come in," Trina
called.

Her mother and Martin stuck their heads in.
"Just wanted to say good night," Martin said.

"Good night," the girls chorused.

"Is everything working out in here?" Laura
asked. "Do you like sharing the room?"

"It's just fine," Sarah said.

"Perfect," Trina assured them.

Laura blew kisses at them. Then they closed the door.

Trina pulled the covers up and shut her eyes tightly. She just hoped Sarah wouldn't go on reading too long.

Chapter 6

Two days later, coming home from school, Sarah was not in a very good mood. Nothing bad had happened at school. It was the thought of going home that was getting her down.

It wasn't that she didn't like her home or her parents or Trina. Her feelings came from a peculiar discovery she'd made, something that had been gradually dawning on her. Sharing a room wasn't anywhere near as easy as she'd thought it would be. It was *tiring*.

With Trina in the room, Sarah felt that a conversation had to be going on all the time. Sometimes, it was impossible to find anything to talk about. When that happened, Sarah felt like at least she had to smile.

By now, her lips had been stretched out from all those forced smiles. But what else could she do? It wouldn't be nice to be in the same room with another person and not talk or smile. The other person might think you didn't want her there.

The real problem was having to be so nice all the time. It was *exhausting*. Sarah had been surprised to discover that fact. She'd always thought she was a basically nice person. At Camp Sunnyside, she'd never had any problems sharing a cabin and getting along with all her cabin mates. She couldn't remember ever being tired there.

Then why was she so exhausted now? It didn't make any sense to her at all.

Of course, things were different at camp. You could act totally natural there. You didn't have to worry about ruining your parents' marriage.

She forced herself to think about something else. It didn't take long for her to come up with another problem—the essay she was writing for her annual school essay competition. Laura had helped her come up with a great topic—Families Today.

She'd done a bunch of research at the library, and she'd gathered tons of information about divorce rates, single-parent families, adoption—all kinds of stuff. But she was having a hard time getting started on the actual writing.

And that brought her back to the problems of sharing a room. How could a person do any serious writing there when you had to talk and smile at another person?

As she climbed the stairs to her bedroom, she became aware of a sense of dread, knowing Trina would already be there. She just didn't feel like talking or smiling or being nice right this minute.

So when she opened the door, and saw that the room was empty, she breathed an enormous sigh of relief, and plopped down on her bed. She decided to relax for a few minutes before starting her essay, and reached for the book she'd left lying open on the bed last night.

But it wasn't there.

"Trina," Sarah muttered. She hauled herself off the bed and went to the bookcase. This time she had to really search to find her book. When she finally located it and pulled it out, she groaned. Since she'd left it open on her bed, she hadn't bothered to put a bookmark in it. Trina had closed it to put it away, and lost her place.

For a second, Sarah had an enormous urge to throw something across the room. Calm down, she ordered herself. Get to work on your essay.

But first, she had to get out of her school

clothes. She knelt down on the floor to retrieve the jeans and sweatshirt she'd left under her bed yesterday. She pushed her arm in as far as it would go and moved it around, but she felt nothing there. Then she lay her head on the floor and peered. There was nothing under her bed.

Sarah clenched her teeth. She had a pretty good suspicion she knew what had happened to her jeans and sweatshirt.

"Sarah? What are you doing on the floor?"

Sarah struggled to her feet and managed to smile at Laura. "Nothing. Just looking for something. Where's Trina?"

"I just dropped her off at gymnastics practice." Laura leaned against the door frame and gazed at Sarah thoughtfully. "How's everything going between you two? Are you still happy about sharing a room?"

Hardly, Sarah thought. But aloud, she said, "Yeah, sure, it's great. Sharing is fun. It's nice having company all the time." She was amazed at how smoothly she was able to lie.

"No problems?"

"None at all," Sarah assured her.

"Are you sure?"

Sarah began to wonder if she was that good a liar after all. "Why do you keep asking that?"

Laura smiled. "You don't look very happy."

"I was just thinking about this essay I told you about. The one I'm doing for the school competition. I just can't seem to get started on it."

"I don't want to interfere," Laura said, "but if you'd like any help—"

"I'd love some help," Sarah replied promptly.

"Come on down to the kitchen," Laura invited her.

Sarah grabbed her notebooks. "Why are you always working in the kitchen?" she asked Laura as they went down the stairs. "I mean, you've got an office."

"I know." Laura laughed. "It's crazy, right? Here I've got a whole room to use as an office. I go in there every morning, prepared to write, and end up dragging all my stuff into the kitchen."

"Don't you like your office?"

"Oh, it's fine. But I love writing in the kitchen. It's warm and cozy and there are lots of windows to let in light. I can spread my stuff all over the table."

Sarah understood completely. *She* always liked spreading stuff out. Of course, on that new skinny desk in her room, she didn't have much space to do that. Not like she'd been able to do on the big, old desk she'd had before.

They sat down at the kitchen table, and Sarah opened her notebook. "See, I've done all this research on families. I've got divorce rates and all that."

"That's good," Laura said. "But don't get bogged down in statistics. This is a subject you can deal with on an emotional level."

"What do you mean?"

Laura considered this. "Well, the word 'family' has a lot of meanings nowadays. There aren't as many traditional families, with a father and a mother and children who were actually born to them. There are more people coming together as families later in life."

"Like us," Sarah said.

"Exactly. And sometimes kids have a hard time adjusting to this."

"But not like us."

Laura cocked her head to one side. "That's interesting, isn't it? After all, you and Trina are very different—"

"Not really," Sarah interrupted. "It's not like we disagree about anything."

There was an odd expression on Laura's face as she said, "No, you don't, do you?"

Something about her gaze made Sarah shift around in her chair. She sensed that if she told Laura what she was really feeling, Laura would understand. But admitting to those feelings could be dangerous.

She gathered her stuff. "You've been a big help," she told Laura. "I think I can get started on this now."

She went back up to her room. Her mood had improved. Laura was so terrific. At least she didn't have a step*mother* problem.

Sitting down at her desk, she turned on the radio. Music always helped her feel more creative. She opened her notebook and began to write.

When Trina opened the bedroom door, the music hit her like a ton of bricks. "Hi," she called loudly.

Sarah looked over her shoulder. "Hi. How was gymnastics?"

"Fine. What are you doing?"

"Writing my essay for the school competition."

How could she write with that music blaring?

Trina wondered. "I've got lots of math to do," she said. She went to her desk and sat down.

This is good, she thought, doing homework side by side. They were together, but they wouldn't have to make conversation or keep smiles on their faces. Lately, her jaws had been aching from all that smiling.

But she couldn't think with that music going on. She looked at Sarah. "Why are you still in your school clothes?"

"I couldn't find my jeans and my sweatshirt."

"The ones you left under the bed?"

Sarah nodded. Her smile was a little stiff. "I guess you must have put them away." She got up and started toward the dresser.

"They're not in there," Trina said. "Since they'd been on the floor, I figured they were dirty. So I put them in the clothes hamper in the bathroom."

Sarah didn't even thank her. She yanked open her dresser drawer. "I'll have to find something else," she mumbled.

Trina turned her attention back to the math problems. But it was hopeless. There was no way she could concentrate with that music. And she didn't dare ask Sarah to turn it off. She didn't seem to be in a very good mood.

"I think I'll go see if I can help with dinner," she murmured. Sarah didn't respond.

Down in the kitchen, Trina found her stepfather chopping onions. "What are you making?"

"Only the most phenomenal lasagna you ever tasted," Martin replied.

"Can I help?"

"Hmm, let me think about that," he mused. "If I allow you to assist me, you'll learn all my secret ingredients."

Trina raised her right hand. "I solemnly swear never to reveal your secrets."

Martin grinned at her. "Well, if you can't trust a family member, who can you trust? Let's see . . . do you know how to grate cheese?"

Trina grinned back at him. "I think I can figure that out."

It was nice and cozy, working together in the kitchen. "How's everything going?" Martin asked.

"Great," Trina said. "Everything's perfect."

"I can't get over you and Sarah," he said.

"What do you mean?"

"You two get along so well!"

"What's surprising about that?" Trina asked.

"I'm thinking of all the little spats she and

Alison used to have," Martin noted. "And they weren't even sharing a room!"

Trina didn't know what to say. She wasn't surprised that Sarah and Alison had arguments. They didn't have to worry about destroying a family.

"You know," Martin continued, "when I was a boy, I shared a room with my younger brother. It wasn't always easy. I would have given anything for my own room, but our house was too small."

The conversation was making Trina uncomfortable. "I've finished grating the cheese. What can I do next?"

"How are you at boiling water?" Martin asked.

Trina laughed. "That's my specialty!"

Dr. Fine wasn't kidding when he said his lasagna was phenomenal.

"Martin, this is heaven!" Laura exclaimed. "Boy, did I luck out on choosing a husband!"

Martin rolled his eyes. "I knew it," he said. "She only married me for my cooking. By the way, I hate to tell you all this, but I'm on call at the hospital this weekend. So I'm afraid we can't plan any big family outings."

"It's just as well." Laura sighed. "I'll be chained to my word processor all weekend if I'm going to finish this article by Monday."

"Do you girls have any plans?" Martin asked.

Trina and Sarah looked at each other. "Is there anything special you'd like to do?" Trina asked politely.

"What would *you* like to do?" Sarah countered in a voice that was just as polite.

Laura looked at them quizzically. "You know, you two don't have to do everything together."

"But we want to," Sarah said.

"Really, we do," Trina agreed. "Sarah, you choose."

"I haven't been to the Glenwood public library yet," Sarah said. "We could do that."

That didn't seem too thrilling to Trina. She wanted to do something more active. But she wouldn't mind checking out a book to read, and that couldn't take very long. Maybe they could do something else afterwards. "Okay, that sounds good to me."

After dinner, it was Sarah's turn to do the dishes, so Trina headed back up to her room. With some privacy and quiet, she could do her math and maybe even have time to write in her diary.

But when she walked into the room, she was appalled. How did Sarah manage to create such a mess in such a short period of time? Her clothes were all over the place. Crumpled sheets of paper lay on the floor around her desk. The remains of a candy bar wrapper lay on her bed.

Trina knew she couldn't work in that chaos. She began picking up Sarah's clothes. She gathered the crumpled papers and the candy bar wrapper and threw them away. She stacked Sarah's books neatly on her desk.

And all the while, she seethed. She was turning into Sarah's personal maid!

As soon as she was finished, she grabbed her diary. She wrote fast and furiously. *Sarah can be such a pig! This room looks like a disaster all the time. I've got to make her start being neater or I'll go nuts!*

That was all she managed to get down before Sarah returned. Trina slammed the notebook shut and put it back on her nightstand.

Sarah went to her desk. "Hey, what happened here?"

"I neatened it up a bit for you," Trina replied.

Once again, Sarah didn't thank her. She didn't even *look* pleased. "Um, I had things in a certain order."

Trina tried to keep her tone even. "It didn't look very orderly to me."

Sarah looked around. "What happened to my school clothes?"

"I put them away. I guess you were in a rush and didn't have time to pick up after yourself."

Sarah shrugged. "I guess I'm just a naturally sloppy person."

Trina swallowed. "I guess I'm just naturally neat." She stretched her lips into something like a smile. So did Sarah.

But Sarah's face didn't look very happy. And Trina suspected her own didn't, either.

Chapter 7

The next morning, while Trina was down-stairs doing the breakfast dishes, Sarah sprawled on her unmade bed and finished her letter to Megan. She signed it, and then she went back to her desk for an envelope. She searched through the piles of papers and books and notepads on her desk top, and then rummaged through the drawers.

"Darn," she muttered. She went to Trina's desk and opened a drawer.

Trina walked into the room. "What are you doing?" she asked sharply.

"Looking for an envelope," Sarah replied.

Trina came over to the desk and closed the drawer Sarah had opened. Then she opened another. As Sarah might have guessed, there was a neat little row of envelopes. "All you had to do was ask me," Trina said.

"Thanks." Sarah took the envelope and tossed it on her desk. She'd address it later. "Ready to go to the library?"

"Aren't you going to make your bed?" Trina asked.

"Later," Sarah replied.

Trina's lips tightened, but she didn't say anything. They left the house, and started up the block. As they walked, Sarah tried to think of some topic of conversation. Why had talking become such a problem? Back at Camp Sunnyside, the girls couldn't *stop* talking. There were many times when their counselor, Carolyn, had to yell at them to shut up after lights out. Now, here they were, with absolutely nothing to say.

They passed some shops, a roller-skating rink, and a fire station. "Here's the library," Sarah said.

It was a small brick building, with white columns in front. Inside, Sarah looked around curiously. Then she sighed in contentment. It was just the kind of public library she liked, cozy and cluttered.

Trina paused at a cart labeled New Books for Young Adults. "This looks good," she said. Sarah glanced at the title. It was a biography of some famous woman tennis player. Not exactly *her* idea of fun reading.

"What are you going to get?" Trina asked.

"I don't know. I have to look around." Sarah's spirits lifted. She could spend hours in a place like this.

Trina sat at one of the library tables and drummed her fingers on the top. She had checked out her book, but she wasn't in the mood for reading it right that minute. She was ready to move on and do something else.

But Sarah hadn't even picked out a book yet. Trina watched her browsing through the shelves. She'd pull off a book and stand there, reading a few pages. Then she'd put it back.

If she kept on doing that, they'd be there all day! Trina thought longingly of the roller rink they'd passed on the way. That's where *she* wanted to be.

Restless and bored, she got up and joined Sarah. "Found anything good yet?"

"Sure, lots of stuff. I could stay here all day."

"You could?"

She tried to keep the dismay out of her voice, but Sarah picked up on it. "You want to leave?"

"I don't mind staying. I was just thinking . . ."

"What?"

"Maybe we could go to the roller rink when you're done."

"The roller rink?" Sarah made a face.

"We don't *have* to," Trina said.

There was a moment of silence. "Yeah, okay. Let me just choose a book."

That took another fifteen minutes. Trina waited for her by the exit.

"I'm ready," Sarah said. "Let's go."

In Trina's opinion, from the way she said that, you'd have thought they were going to the dentist.

Lacing up her skates, Sarah wished there was a way she could skate and read at the same time. Since she could barely stay on her feet when she skated, she decided that wouldn't be a very good idea.

But roller skating was so boring, she thought. You just went 'round and 'round in circles. Not to mention the fact that she'd be risking two skinned knees.

Side by side, she and Trina began skating. It wasn't easy staying together, though. Trina's legs were longer and she was a much better skater. She kept moving ahead, then pausing, waiting for Sarah to catch up. Sarah didn't think Trina could be having much fun.

Well, that was too bad for her, Sarah thought. It wasn't much fun for Sarah either.

They went around the rink. Sarah tripped three times and bumped into at least five other skaters. By the time they circled the rink twice, Sarah was ready to give up roller skating for life.

"Oh, wow!" Trina exclaimed suddenly. "Some girls I know are over there. Come on!"

Trina zoomed off. It took Sarah longer to get there. By then, Trina and the two girls were already engaged in animated conversation. Trina paused to introduce her. "Janie, Beth, this is my stepsister, Sarah."

Sarah bristled. Hadn't they agreed to call each other sisters? "Nice to meet you," she mumbled.

"Janie and Beth take gymnastics with me," Trina said. "And they live right here in Glenwood! I didn't know that. Janie, you were super on the beam yesterday. How did you manage to keep your balance?"

"I haven't the slightest idea!" Janie said. "I just pretended I had glue on my shoes! But I'm having real problems with the parallel bars."

They all started talking about gymnastics. It was like a foreign language to Sarah. Personally, she thought it was rude of Trina to talk about something she knew Sarah wasn't interested in at all.

"Let's form a line and skate together," Beth suggested.

"Great!" Trina exclaimed. She grabbed Sarah's hand and they all took off.

"I can't keep up!" Sarah protested. But no one heard her. They dragged her along, pulling her faster than her legs could move. She jerked her hand away from Trina's, lost her balance, and fell down.

The girls gathered around her. "Are you okay?" Trina asked. At least she had the courtesy to fake a little concern.

Sarah got up. "Yeah, I'm okay. Listen, Trina, I have to go home. I just remembered that some friends from school were going to the movies in Glenwood this afternoon and I asked them to stop by afterwards if they had time."

"You did?"

"You don't have to come with me." Sarah actually hoped she wouldn't. But she wondered what their parents would think if she showed up home alone. Would they worry that she and Trina had had a fight?

The same thought seemed to occur to Trina. "I'll go with you. See you guys later."

Once again, there didn't seem to be much to talk about on the way home. But Trina seemed more cheerful. "That was fun," Trina said. "I'm so glad Janie and Beth live around here. We can hang out with them."

"Yeah," Sarah said. "Great."

Laura and Martin were in the kitchen when the girls arrived home. "Did you two have a good time?" Laura asked.

"Yeah," Sarah said.

"Super," Trina added, keeping her face averted from her mother's eyes. Sarah was really starting to annoy her, and she was afraid it would show.

Trina had gone to the library without complaining. At least she'd pretended to enjoy it. But Sarah hadn't even tried to have fun at the roller rink. She'd been practically rude to Trina's friends.

And now she'd invited *her* friends to their home without even telling Trina. That wasn't very polite.

"Hungry?" Martin asked. "Want something to eat?"

"No thanks," Trina replied.

"I'm hungry," Sarah said. She went to the refrigerator. Trina headed upstairs.

In the bedroom, she shook her head wearily as she eyed Sarah's unmade bed. Surely she'd want it to look neat before her friends came. She picked up a paper off the bed. The heading caught her eye—*Dear Megan.* Then she saw her own name farther down the page.

It wasn't right to read another person's letter. But with her own name on it . . .

Her eyes widened as she read. *Trina is getting on my nerves. I don't know what I'm going to do. It's really hard being sisters. I don't even know if we can keep on being friends.*

So that was how Sarah felt about her! Trina felt cold shivers run up and down her spine. Her stomach turned over. Then the cold shivers turned into hot flashes of anger. For once, she didn't even think about her parents and their marriage. All she could think about was herself—and how she could manage to go on living with this person.

* * *

106

Sarah and her friends Ellen and Karen sat on her bed eating cookies and playing Scrabble.

"This house is super," Karen told Sarah.

"And I really like your new mother," Ellen said. "I'm not so sure about your sister."

"*Step*sister," Sarah corrected her. She wasn't surprised by Ellen's reaction. When the girls had arrived a couple of hours earlier, Sarah had introduced them to Trina. Trina had been polite but not friendly at all. And she'd refused their invitation to play Scrabble.

"Where did she go, anyway?" Karen asked.

"I think she's in the den." Sarah was glad her father had gone to the hospital and Laura was at the supermarket.

"Come on, Ellen, it's your turn," Karen said.

"It's going to take me a while," Ellen replied. "I've got bad letters."

Karen got up off the bed and wandered around the room, ending up on Trina's side. "Gee, is she ever tidy."

Sarah glanced up. Karen was standing by Trina's nightstand, and she picked up the notebook lying there.

"Um, Karen, I think that's her diary."

That didn't bother Karen. She opened the notebook. "Wow! I can't believe this!"

Sarah opened her mouth to protest. After all, nobody should read another person's diary.

But Karen hadn't finished. "Listen to what she wrote about you!"

Karen began to read. And by the time she finished, Sarah no longer wanted to protect Trina's privacy.

"She called me a pig?"

"That's what it says right here."

Ellen gasped. "Oh, Sarah. How awful! You must feel so hurt!"

But Sarah was too furious to feel anything else.

Trina sat curled up on the couch in the den. The TV was on, but she wasn't really watching it. She knew Sarah's friends had left, but she didn't feel like going back up to the bedroom.

Then, through a window, she saw Martin's car pulling into the driveway. He'd wonder why Trina was down here alone. Reluctantly, she got off the couch and ran upstairs.

Sarah didn't even look up when she came into the bedroom. Passing her, Trina said, "There are crumbs all over your bed."

"Of course there are," Sarah replied. "After all, I'm a pig, right?"

Trina gazed at her in bewilderment. Then she noticed that her diary had been moved from the nightstand to her bed. She gasped. "You read my diary!"

Sarah didn't say anything, but she wouldn't look Trina in the face. Trina clenched her fists.

"You know, Sarah, I think you're right. I don't think we can even be friends, let alone sisters."

Now it was Sarah's turn to gasp. "You read my letter to Megan!"

"How could I help it? You left it lying on your bed! If you put things away—"

Sarah interrupted. "Yeah? Well, maybe you better stop messing with my things!"

"Messing with *your* things?" Trina could hear her voice rising but she couldn't help it. "You took my marking pens without even asking! You were poking around in my desk drawer just this morning!"

"What's the matter?" Sarah asked sarcastically. "Afraid I might make a mess of your desk drawer?" Her voice was getting louder too.

"You make a mess of everything else! And I can't live in a mess!"

"Well, I can't live with you!" Sarah shot back.

"Sarah! Trina!"

Trina whirled around. There was horror on Sarah's face. And for good reason.

Their parents were standing in the doorway.

Chapter 8

Martin looked amazed. Laura's face was stricken. Both of the girls were stunned into silence.

Trina recovered first. "Oh, Mom, Martin, I'm sorry!"

"Me too!" Sarah cried out. "We weren't really fighting, you know."

"Really, everything's fine!" Trina insisted.

Their parents didn't actually look angry or even terribly upset. But they were both obviously bewildered.

"I don't think everything's fine at all," Dr. Fine said. "And I think we should talk about this."

"Let's go down to the den," Laura said.

Trina could feel her heart thumping with every step down the stairs. She felt sick. How could she have been so selfish? Her mother had been so happy—and now Trina had ruined everything. If only she could have gone on pretending!

She took a sideways glance at Sarah. Sarah's face was pale, and she looked sick too.

"Now," Martin said, sitting on the couch. "What's going on here?"

Miserable, Trina considered denying that any problems existed. But it was no use anymore. She looked at Sarah, hoping she'd speak first.

Sarah didn't speak. She burst into tears. "It's all my fault," she cried.

The tears were contagious. "No, no," Trina wept. "It's my fault."

"I have a feeling it's not anybody's fault," her mother said. "Why don't you just tell us what you were fighting about and maybe we can help you work it out."

Sarah sniffed. "We weren't actually fighting," she mumbled feebly.

"Stop that," her father ordered her. "I can recognize an argument when I hear one! Why do you two keep denying it?"

"It's normal to disagree," Laura added. She picked up a box of tissues and passed it around.

"That's right," Dr. Fine said. "Sarah, you and Alison argue all the time."

"That's different," Sarah said.

"Why?" Laura asked.

"We're *real* sisters. We don't *have* to get along."

Laura looked at Martin. "I'm very confused."

"So am I. Why is it okay for you to argue with Alison and not with Trina?"

Sarah was busy blowing her nose so Trina spoke up for the both of them. "We don't want to fight. *Ever.*"

"But that's impossible," her mother said. "Everyone disagrees some of the time."

"But we can't," Sarah said. "Not if we want you two to say together."

"And we do," Trina added.

"Now I'm even more confused," Laura said. "What do your arguments have to do with our marriage?"

Sarah raised her tear-stained face. "Many second marriages break up because the step-children don't get along. I read that when I was doing research for my essay."

Trina nodded. "And I know a girl whose parents got divorced because she didn't get along with her stepsister."

Understanding seemed to hit both parents at the same time. "Good grief," Dr. Fine said. "So *that's* it. That's why you two have been knocking yourselves out trying to show us how well you get along."

The girls nodded.

"And that's why you insisted on sharing a room when you each could have had your own," Laura said.

Again, they nodded.

"Oh, girls." Sarah's father sighed. "Nobody expects you to be *that* compatible. We know you love each other. But you're two different people, with different interests and different tastes and different habits."

"No kidding," Trina murmured, thinking about their bedroom.

Her mother must have been reading her mind. "First of all, I think you should each have your own room."

"But what about your office?" Sarah asked.

Laura smiled. "That's a total waste of space. Like I told you, I always end up working in the kitchen. And I can use the pantry for my files."

"And you don't have to do everything together all the time," Dr. Fine noted.

"You mean, I don't have to go roller skating?" Sarah murmured.

"And I don't have to hang around the library all day?" Trina asked.

"Of course not!" Martin exclaimed.

"You can have different friends, too," Laura said. "Sarah, you just said you don't always get along with Alison, right? Because you're real sisters?"

Sarah nodded.

"Well, I think you and Trina should try being real sisters, too," Martin stated. "Girls, you are hereby permitted to disagree and argue and even fight."

"Not too often, I hope," Laura put in. "But even if you do, we'll still love you."

"And you'll still love each other?" Trina asked.

Martin was looking at his wife when he answered that. "Absolutely."

That was the cue for a series of hugs. When they all finally released one another, Sarah turned to Trina. "You know what I think? I bet we'll get along a whole lot better when we stop trying to get along. If you know what I mean."

"I know exactly what you mean." Trina gave the adults an abashed smile. "I guess I just wanted us to be a perfect family."

Her mother stroked her head. "Honey, there's no such thing."

"But we can be a *real* family," Martin said. "How does that sound to you?"

Sarah and Trina looked at each other. They grinned. And in unison, they both exclaimed, "Perfect!"